ANTY HERO

BARRY HUTCHISON

WITH ILLUSTRATIONS BY
TOM PERCIVAL

Barrington Stoke

First published in 2018 in Great Britain by
Barrington Stoke Ltd
18 Walker Street, Edinburgh, EH3 7LP

www.barringtonstoke.co.uk

A CIP catalogue record for this book is available
from the British Library upon request

ISBN: 978-1-78112-836-7

Printed in China by Leo

Contents

Chapter 1
Eye Surprise

Zac was kneeling on the grass in the school garden. He had a pile of seeds cupped in his hands and the class weirdo squatting beside him.

Zac had been the class weirdo for a while, thanks to his love of country and western music, Korean movies and comic books from the 1950s. Back then, he'd had a friend list of zero. But then Ant had started at the school, and Zac was no longer the weirdest kid in the class.

There was something very odd about Ant. A number of odd things, if you looked closely enough.

First of all, his sunglasses with huge round dark-green lenses. Ant said he had to wear them all the time because his eyes were sensitive to light. Most of the other kids in his classes reckoned Ant was just trying to look cool. But if that was true, he was failing badly. Ant didn't look cool at all.

He was the opposite of cool. Ant was short and skinny with a head that was too large for his body. His fingers were long and bony, and he always looked like he needed a wash – with a power hose.

On Ant's first day at the school, an older girl had spotted a cockroach crawling in his hair and screamed until she was sick. Ant hadn't had much of a chance after that. Some mean kids called him names like "Roach Head" and "Bug Boy". Most of the others just kept out

of Ant's way or whispered about him whenever he entered the room. Apart from Zac. As soon as Ant had arrived, he and Zac bonded over their weirdness, and Zac's friend list grew from zero to one.

Ant squatted beside Zac and prodded seeds into a hole in the soil.

"Nice work," Zac said, and handed Ant another seed. "Oh, I meant to ask," Zac added, "what are you up to after school?"

"I do not know," said Ant as he popped the seed into a hole. "Why do you ask this?"

Ant's accent was another odd thing about him. It was like no accent Zac had ever heard before. Whenever anyone asked Ant where he came from, he just shrugged and told them, "Somewhere south".

"Just thought you might fancy a game of footie," Zac said.

Ant's eyebrows dipped into a frown behind his huge sunglasses. "What is 'footie'?" Ant asked.

"Footie," Zac repeated, as if that word explained everything. Zac soon realised that it hadn't and he carried on. "Football. You know, a kick-about?"

Ant still looked confused. Zac laughed and said, "Wait, you've never heard of *football*?"

Ant shook his head and turned back to the seeds. Zac was about to ask Ant if he was being serious, but the teacher's voice butted in.

"Remember, each seed must be at least eight centimetres apart if we want a successful crop," Mr Dawkin told them. He mopped his shiny forehead and glanced up at the hot sun. "And don't forget to water them," Mr Dawkin added.

Ant looked up at Zac, making the light glint off the dark-green lenses of his glasses. "What is 'eight centimetres'?" Ant asked.

Zac wasn't great with measurements. He held his two index fingers apart, guessing eight centimetres. "About that," he said.

"Miles off," a voice from behind them said. It was Tulisa, the third member of their team on the "Seed to Supper" science project. She had grabbed the only watering can before anyone else could get their hands on it, then come over to join Zac and Ant. Tulisa nodded down at Zac's fingers and said, "Closer."

Zac moved his fingers together until they almost touched. Tulisa sighed. "Not *that* close."

She set the watering can down on the ground and used her own fingers to show how big eight centimetres was. It was almost exactly how far apart Ant and Zac had been sowing the seeds anyway.

While Tulisa's back was turned, someone from the nearest group grabbed the watering can. The boy yanked it away before Tulisa could stop him.

"Give it back, Ray," Tulisa said. "We're using that."

"No, you weren't," Ray replied. He was the biggest kid in their class and liked to boss the others around. Most of the time he got away with it because he was Mr Dawkin's son.

Zac stood up beside Tulisa. He wasn't sure whether Ant hadn't seen what was going on or that Ant didn't care. He had a sort of dreamy half-smile on his face as he wriggled his fingers around in the soil.

"We need the watering can, Ray," Zac said. "We were just about to use it."

"For what?" asked Ray. "To give Bug Boy a shower? You should – he stinks!"

"What's going on here?" Mr Dawkin demanded as he trudged across the garden.

"Ray took our watering can," Zac said.

Mr Dawkin raised one of his grey eyebrows. "*Your* watering can?" he said. "I'm sorry, Zac, did you pay for it? Did you bring it from home?"

"Well, no," Zac admitted. "But we got it first, and—"

"No," Mr Dawkin said, cutting Zac off. "Then Ray is free to use it, isn't he?"

"Yes, sir. Suppose," Zac mumbled.

"Oh, toughen up, boy," Mr Dawkin spat. "It's not like it's the end of the world."

"Sorry, sir," Zac said.

Tulisa glared at Mr Dawkin for a moment, then leaned past him and stared at Ray. "We're next with it," Tulisa said. "Don't be long."

Ray grinned, which showed off his yellow teeth. "Yeah, right," Ray said.

A high-pitched scream of terror came from across the garden. Everyone – even Ant – looked round to see Molly dancing on the spot, swatting at herself and squealing.

"Ew, ew, ew!" Molly yelled. "Bugs. There are bugs on everything!"

"It's just greenfly," Mr Dawkin said. He flicked one of the tiny green insects off Molly's arm and added, "They're harmless, and really quite fascinating in their own way."

"Kill them, Dad!" Ray cackled. "Use your spray."

"Yes. Yes, good idea," Mr Dawkin said. "Don't want them spoiling the crops."

He unclipped a spray bottle from his belt and sprayed bright-blue liquid at a row of plants near Molly's feet.

Ant sprang up as if he'd been electrocuted. "Wait, stop!" Ant cried. He stumbled into Zac, and they both tumbled to the ground.

"Watch it!" Zac yelled, but he was already flat on his back. He rolled out from under Ant, and that was when he saw it.

The weirdest thing about Ant. Maybe the weirdest thing he'd ever seen.

Ant's sunglasses had been knocked off as he'd fallen, and it was the first time Zac had seen his eyes. They were big, wide and made up of hundreds of lenses. As Zac looked into them, hundreds of identical versions of his own face were reflected back at him. Ant's eyes weren't human. They were bug eyes!

"Whoa," Zac whispered.

And that was when the screaming started.

Chapter 2
The Shocking Truth

At first, Zac thought the screaming was because someone else had seen Ant's eyes. But then Molly started dancing around again and yelling that the greenflies were trying to climb inside her ears.

Ant grabbed his glasses and covered his eyes while everyone was distracted by Molly. The hundreds of Zacs became just two again in the green lenses of Ant's sunglasses.

"Um ..." Zac said. It was pretty much the only thing his brain could think of. "Um ..."

Ant cleared his throat and gave a twitchy smile. "What?" he said, looking nervous. "Is there a problem?"

Zac just blinked as he thought of the sight of Ant's bug eyes. "Um ..."

"Yes, there's a problem," Tulisa hissed. "You've got eyes like a spider's!"

Ant shook his head. "No," he said. "You are mistaken."

"No, we *aren't*," Tulisa replied. She nudged Zac and said, "Tell him."

"Um ..." Zac began.

"Most spiders have eight eyes that they cannot move," Ant said. He sounded quite calm and normal. "My eyes are not like that."

Tulisa tutted. "OK, well ... eyes like a *fly's*, then."

"That is more accurate, yes," Ant said. He turned his head and glanced around at the rest of the class. Everyone seemed to be focusing on the screaming Molly – apart from Mr Dawkin, who was watching Ant, Zac and Tulisa.

Ant lowered his voice to a whisper and said, "Please. Do not tell the others. It would not end well for me."

Tulisa crossed her arms and rocked back on her heels. "Fine. Then explain," she demanded, elbowing Zac in the ribs. "And stop just standing there with your mouth open."

Zac closed his mouth. "But ... but ..." he said. It was better than "Um", but not by much.

"After school. I will explain then," Ant whispered. "We can meet over by the garage for bicycles."

"You mean the bike sheds?" Tulisa said. "Fine. But you'd better spill the beans."

Ant frowned. "I do not have beans."

"I mean you'd better explain," Tulisa said. "Or I'll tell everyone about your eye thing."

"Oh. Yes. I will," Ant promised.

"And don't be late!" Tulisa told him.

*

Zac and Tulisa stood behind the bike sheds and checked the time on their phones. "He's not coming," Tulisa said.

"Give him another few minutes," Zac told her. He'd finally got over his shock at seeing Ant's eyes, but it had taken until fifth period. "He'll be here," Zac added.

Tulisa tutted. "Nah. He's not coming," she said. She turned to leave and saw Ant standing behind them with a wide smile on his face.

"How long have you been there for?" Tulisa demanded.

"Eleven minutes," Ant said. "You said not to be late."

"So you've been standing there in silence the whole time?" Zac asked.

Ant nodded.

Tulisa rolled her eyes and sighed. "You're *such* a weirdo!"

Zac thought that standing in silence behind them was actually the least weird thing about Ant. But Tulisa was pretty scary, so Zac didn't say anything in case it annoyed her.

"Now spill," Tulisa said to Ant. "What's wrong with your eyes?"

"Nothing," Ant replied.

Zac and Tulisa looked at each other.

"Uh, yes there is," Zac said.

"No, my eyes are normal," Ant insisted. "Where I come from, lots of us have eyes like this."

Ant pushed the glasses up onto his head, and Zac saw his own surprised reflection in each of the hundreds of tiny lenses.

"What do you mean 'where you come from'?" Zac asked. "I thought you came from somewhere south."

"I do. Sort of," Ant said. He pointed at the ground. "I come from down there."

Zac blinked. "What? Underground? I thought by 'south' that you meant France or somewhere."

"What is 'France'?" Ant asked.

"Doesn't matter," Tulisa snapped. "So let me get this right. You have bug eyes, come from somewhere underground and there are more people like you down there?"

"Not exactly like me," Ant said. He frowned, and his big round eyes narrowed into ovals. "I am ... different."

"You can say that again," Tulisa agreed.

"But I have friends," Ant said. His smile returned. "They would like to say hello to you."

Zac and Tulisa looked around. School had finished twenty minutes ago. Other than the three of them, there was no one about.

"Where are these friends?" Zac asked.

Ant pointed downwards again. Tulisa and Zac followed his finger, then both gasped. Critters of all shapes and sizes were climbing up from cracks in the ground. Spiders scurried,

worms wiggled and ants advanced. Soon the area around Ant's feet looked like a thick carpet of bugs.

"Zac, Tulisa, meet my friends," Ant said. "Or some of them, anyway. There are lots more." His smile grew wider. "I'm much more popular where I come from than I am here."

Zac said nothing. He couldn't. His whole body was frozen as he stared at all the bugs wriggling and squirming together. Zac felt as if his skin was trying to climb up onto his head to get away from the critters. If he could have moved his legs, he would have run away, but his feet were stuck to the spot.

"B-bugs," Zac said.

"Well spotted," Tulisa replied. She didn't sound as scared as Zac, but she seemed uneasy. "A *lot* of bugs."

"They're all harmless," Ant told them. "Apart from Brian – he has a bit of a temper. But don't worry, his buzz is worse than his bite."

Zac still couldn't speak. Ant turned to him, saw his frozen face and gave a small wave of his hand. Right away, all the bugs burrowed and squirmed back underground.

"Are you OK?" Ant asked.

"I'm pretty far from *OK*!" Zac said in a voice that was just a squeak. "You're a ... you're a ... Well, I don't know what you are, but you're not human. Or are you?" Zac shook his head and added, "No, you can't be. Or can you?"

"I am not human," Ant said. "But nor am I a bug. I am somewhere between the two."

"How is that possible?" Tulisa asked.

Ant shrugged. "I do not know. I lived down there for many years. Then an earwig called Jennifer told me about the world up here. I watched people for a while. I learned your language and some of your traditions. One day, I came to investigate further."

"Why did you come to school?" Tulisa asked. "Why would you do that to yourself?"

"I wished to learn more of your ways," Ant said. He shrugged. "But now I must return. It is no longer safe for me here."

Ant thrust out a hand to Zac, which scared Zac so much that he screamed. He saw Ant's shocked face and managed to pull himself together. Bug person or not, Ant was still his friend, and Zac didn't want to hurt his feelings.

"Goodbye, Zac," Ant said. "I am sorry we did not get to kick about the footie."

"Uh, yeah," Zac said as he forced himself to shake Ant's hand. "Yeah, me too."

Ant turned to Tulisa. "You are very frightening," Ant told her. "But you are kinder than you pretend to be."

"Well, you're half right," Tulisa said. She folded her arms. "So what now, Ant? You going to start digging?"

Ant smiled at them both. "Yes," he said. "But not here." He nodded, spun around and walked away.

Zac and Tulisa stood in silence as they watched him stride off across the school grounds. It was Zac who spoke first.

"That did just happen, didn't it?" Zac said. "This isn't a dream?"

Tulisa pinched him on the arm, making him yelp.

"Nope. Not a dream," she said.

As Ant passed close to the school building he stopped and waved. Zac and Tulisa waved back.

"*Such* a weird kid," Tulisa said.

Zac's shock was fading, and he began to feel sadness creeping in. He hadn't known Ant long, but they'd been friends. He was going to miss him, Zac realised.

"Ant will be safer this way," Zac said as he tried to tell himself that it was the best thing for Ant that he left.

Zac and Tulisa both watched as a door near Ant opened. Two big men jumped out, grabbed Ant and dragged him inside.

"Or, you know," Zac said. "Maybe not."

Chapter 3
Bug-napped!

It took just over ten seconds for Zac and Tulisa to reach the door, then another two to realise it had been locked.

Zac raised his fist to knock, but Tulisa stopped him. She put a finger to her lips and moved her ear closer to the door. Zac copied her. They could hear a surly male voice on the other side.

"Ugh, stick that bag over his head," the man said. "He gives me the creeps."

"Too right," said another voice. Zac realised who they were – the school's two lab assistants. "Let's get him up to the lab so Dawkin can do his tests. Then we'll get our money," the second man continued.

There was a *creak* as another door opened, then a *thud* as it closed again. Zac thought he could hear Ant struggling, but the noises were getting further away.

"Mr Dawkin!" Tulisa said. "He must have seen Ant's eyes."

"And now he's going to do 'tests' on him!" Zac cried. "We need to call the police."

"And tell them what?" Tulisa asked. "That our science teacher has bug-napped a human insect? The police would probably lock *us* up for wasting their time."

Zac leaned back and looked up at the windows of the science corridor, two floors up. "Well, we can't just leave him!" Zac said.

"He's a weirdo," Tulisa replied. "But he's *our* weirdo. Of course we're not going to leave him."

"You know, I think that's the nicest thing I've ever heard you say," Zac told her.

"Yeah, yeah, shut up," Tulisa warned Zac. She started jogging around to the front of the building. "Come on, let's find a way in."

*

After a lot of searching, Zac and Tulisa had found an open door near the staff room and sneaked inside. They dodged the cleaners down on the ground floor, sticking close together. At the stairs, they rushed up two at a time as they headed for the science corridor.

But there was someone waiting for them on the first floor. Ray was standing with his arms folded across his broad chest as he blocked the stairs to the second floor.

"Well, well, well, looks like my old man was right," Ray said as he glared at Zac. "He told me you might come after the freak. But I didn't think you'd bring your girlfriend."

"What?" Zac said. "Ha! *Girlfriend?* As if!" He laughed a bit too loudly, then was silent.

"Get out of the way," Tulisa said. She tried to push past Ray, but he didn't move.

"Uh-uh. No way," Ray sneered. "See, my dad told me all about that bug-eyed buddy of yours, and he reckons he's going to make us rich. Discovering a new species is a big deal, you know? Especially when it's a weird half-bug half-human! It'll make my dad famous all over the world. He's going to be minted. *We're* going to be minted."

Ray drew himself up to his full height to tower above them. He cracked his knuckles and said, "So if you two think you're getting past me, you've got another think coming."

The words had barely left Ray's lips when Tulisa's fist slammed into his stomach. The impact pushed them both on for a few metres. Then Ray toppled backwards, and Tulisa crashed down on top of him.

"Get off!" Ray spat. He lashed out and swung a punch at Tulisa's ribs. She might have been smaller than Ray, but she was also faster. She caught his arm and twisted his wrist, and he cried out in pain.

"Zac, go help Ant," Tulisa said.

Zac hopped from foot to foot. "Uh, what about you?" he squeaked. "Shouldn't I stay to help you?"

Tulisa snorted. She blocked another punch from Ray and pinned his hand under her knee. "Does it look like I need help?" Tulisa asked. "Go!"

Zac nodded and hurried up the stairs towards the science corridor. Behind him, Tulisa was snarling at the wriggling Ray.

"Now," she said. "Let's talk about that watering can ..."

Chapter 4
Double Danger

Zac slowed down as he reached the top step of the stairs, and took cover behind the high wooden banister. He leaned out and peeked at Mr Dawkin's classroom. Zac had to bite his lip to stop himself gasping. The two lab assistants were standing guard outside the door and looked terrifying in their heavy overalls.

The men were standing side-on to where Zac was hiding, so they couldn't see him unless they turned their heads. That was the good news. The bad news was there was no way Zac could get into the classroom without walking between them.

Zac shrank back and tried to come up with a plan. But he couldn't focus – his heart was beating too fast and his breathing was too shaky.

"Come on, Zac, think," he whispered to himself. He thumped the back of his head against the banister, looked up and almost screamed. A spider was hanging down from the ceiling above him. Zac felt like it was looking right at him with its eight static eyes.

It was a pretty big spider – not huge like a tarantula, but still large. Zac's first thought was to run away crying. This was also his second, third and fourth thought, but he managed to ignore them all.

Instead, he did something that surprised even himself.

"I need your help," Zac whispered to the spider. "Ant's in trouble."

The spider didn't answer. It didn't move at all, in fact, or give any sign that it had heard Zac speak.

"Yeah, I thought that was a long shot," Zac sighed. "Looks like I'll have to handle this myself."

Zac went over some ideas in his mind. He could run at the men, shouting and screaming, and hope he scared them off. But they were much bigger than he was, and he wasn't really very scary, so he decided that wasn't a great plan.

Zac could run away, but that would mean leaving Ant to whatever Mr Dawkin had planned for him. He couldn't do that.

Then Zac spotted a door just across the corridor – a small storage room. This was where the lab assistants hung around, fixing the science equipment and shouting at any kids who got too close.

A plan popped into Zac's head. It was a risky plan, so he tried to forget it. But it wouldn't go away. Zac realised, to his dismay, that it was the only plan he had.

He glanced up at the spider on the ceiling above him. "Thanks for nothing," he whispered. He made sure the men weren't looking, then Zac darted across the corridor, pulled open the door and hurried into the storage room.

Zac listened for a moment. He was sure he would hear the thunder of footsteps as the men chased after him. But the only sound he could hear was the *thudding* of his own heartbeat. It was so loud he was worried the two men would hear it too, so he backed into the room and silently closed the door.

There wasn't a lot of room for Zac to back into. The storage room was really just a large cupboard with shelves on every wall, an old table and two plastic chairs. Bits of broken equipment lay spread out on the table, and most of the shelves sagged under the weight of chemicals, beakers and other scientific stuff that was piled on top of them.

Come on, where are they? Zac thought. He rummaged in some boxes tucked down at the bottom of a shelving rack. The lab assistants were big, but they were also lazy and often got pupils to carry stuff to and from their room. Zac had heaved a box up here just a few days ago. It had to be here somewhere.

Aha!

Zac tore open the lid and almost cheered when he saw a dozen round wireless speakers neatly packed inside a box.

Bingo!

Zac began to sort through them. The first few didn't have any battery charge, but the fifth one did. It took him a minute to connect his phone to it. That was the easy part. The hard part would be everything that came next.

Zac picked up one of the chairs and opened the door a crack. He saw one of the men looking his way and ducked back inside.

Zac held his breath, counted to ten, then looked out again. The man had gone back to staring ahead. Zac grabbed the chair, scampered across the corridor and crept down a few stairs.

He made sure he was tucked out of sight, then opened a music playlist on his phone and hit *Play*. A loud blast of country and western music came blaring out of the storage room.

Zac cranked up the volume until the sound was so loud that it crackled and buzzed. Over the din, he heard the men shouting and frantic footsteps *thacking*.

Zac ducked low and held his breath. With any luck, both men would run in to check what the noise was. But he had a back-up plan ready in case one of them stayed at the classroom door. Zac flicked to the YouTube app on his phone and tapped out a search.

As Zac had feared, just one of the men appeared at the top of the stairs. His back was to Zac as he threw open the storage room door and stormed inside.

"Who's in here?" he demanded.

Zac tapped a video icon and the country and western music jumped to a scene from a horror movie. A man's scream blasted from out of the speaker and into the corridor, followed by him crying for help.

Now came the other lab assistant. He ran down the corridor with his fists raised.

"What's going on?" he cried as he bounded into the room. Zac lifted himself upwards from his hiding place and saw the man looking his friend up and down. "I thought you were being murdered or something."

"It's this stupid thing!" the first man shouted. He held up the speaker and fumbled with it as Zac ran up the stairs. The man switched it off just before the door shut behind him with a *click*.

Out in the corridor, Zac wedged the back of the chair under the door handle, trapping the men inside.

Zac grinned and shot a look up at the spider. "Not bad, huh?" Zac said, but the spider was nowhere to be seen.

With the coast now clear, Zac hurried along the corridor and threw open the door to Mr Dawkin's classroom.

Bright-blue bug spray hit Zac in the face and he fell, coughing, to the floor.

Chapter 5
Six-legged Army

It took Zac a while to get his breath back and for his eyes to stop stinging. In that time he had been tied to a chair. He struggled at the ropes with his arms and legs, but they held tight.

Mr Dawkin loomed above Zac, sneering down at him. He held the bug spray in his hand like a gun, with the nozzle pointed at Zac.

"Don't make me spray you again," Mr Dawkin said. "I've never tested this stuff on humans. Who knows what the side effects might be?"

Zac leaned sideways so he could see past Mr Dawkin. Ant was in one piece, so that was good. He was also strapped to a table. That was less good.

A trolley had been set up next to Ant. It was loaded with scientific equipment – beakers, test tubes, rubber hoses and a lot of sharp and scary things. It didn't look like any of them had been used yet, which came as a relief.

Mr Dawkin had set a camera up too. It was on a tripod and pointed down at Ant, and Zac guessed it was so Mr Dawkin could take photos of the tests he was planning to carry out.

"Ant!" Zac yelled. "Are you OK? What did he do to you?"

"Not much really," Ant said. "He has just talked a lot. Blah, blah, blah."

"I was explaining my motivation," Mr Dawkin said. He looked annoyed. "So you could better understand why I have to do the things I'm about to—"

"Like that, see?" Ant said. "Blah, blah, blah. He is very boring."

"All right, shut up!" Mr Dawkin hissed. He put down the spray and snatched up a tool that looked like a drill. Zac gulped. "You want me to hurry this up?" Mr Dawkin asked. "Fine, I'll hurry it up!"

"Uh, no," Ant said. He looked very worried all of a sudden. "Please, don't rush."

"Leave him alone!" Zac cried. "Cut it out!"

"Or what?" Mr Dawkin snarled and spun on the spot. "Hmm? What are you going to do about it?" He leaned in close to Zac until he could smell the sour stink of his teacher's sweat.

Something fell onto Mr Dawkin's head and landed in his hair. Zac watched as a spider crept out from the thin grey strands. It seemed to wave a leg, as if it was waving right at Zac.

"What was that?" Mr Dawkin demanded.

He leaned back.

He looked up.

At that moment, thousands of insects poured down from a hole in the ceiling. Mr Dawkin jumped out of the way just in time, and the insects landed on the classroom floor.

"Oh no you don't!" Mr Dawkin snarled as he grabbed for his bug spray.

Mr Dawkin spun around, raised his spray bottle and took aim. He sniggered as he squeezed the trigger. "Bye bye, bugs!" he cried.

"No!" yelped Zac. He leaped to his feet and charged forwards. He was still tied to the chair, but the extra weight came in handy as he slammed into Mr Dawkin's stomach.

Zac's elbow knocked the wind from Mr Dawkin. The bug spray flew across the room as Mr Dawkin stumbled, then fell face-first into the heaving carpet of insects on the floor.

Mr Dawkin screamed as the bugs covered him. Zac let himself fall back down on his seat to watch what happened next.

With a howl, Mr Dawkin clambered to his feet. His entire head and upper body was alive with spiders, beetles, ants, crickets and even a few ladybirds. He ran for the door as he swiped and swatted at himself, but a carpet of ants were marching in under it, blocking his path. Zac guessed there were thousands of the tiny black bugs charging across the floor. Millions, maybe.

Zac shuffled his chair sideways to let the ants pass, then grinned as they climbed up inside the bottom of Mr Dawkin's trouser legs.

"G-get them off!" Mr Dawkin yelled. He grabbed for his bug spray again, but the whole thing was now covered in wasps, and he stopped mid-grab.

The classroom door was thrown wide open, and Tulisa appeared.

"What the heck?!" Tulisa said, then she laughed. "Oh man, look at Dawkin. Those things must really be bugging him! See what I did there? *Bugging*."

"Hilarious," said Zac. "Hurry up and untie us."

"All right, all right, hold your horses," said Tulisa. She picked her way past the armies of bugs and undid the ropes tying Zac to the chair.

Tulisa was about to go and untie Ant, but several bluebottles and a moth had beaten her to it. Ant jumped down from the table, and the carpet of insects gathered around his feet. Wasps and flies circled around his head like his own personal air force.

Part of Zac thought how impressive it looked. The other – much bigger – part was too busy having a panic attack to take it all in.

Ant waved his hands and most of the insects covering Mr Dawkin dropped to the floor or buzzed up into the air. Only the spiders stayed on him. There were hundreds of them. Zac and Tulisa both watched, filled with awe, as the spiders spun webs around the terrified Mr Dawkin. Soon, he was almost fully cocooned, with only his feet and part of his face sticking out of the blanket of white webbing.

"You're not very nice," Ant told Mr Dawkin. "I don't like you. My friends don't like you."

Ant pointed to a butterfly that had just landed on his arm. "And Brian *really* doesn't like you," Ant added. Brian the butterfly fluttered its wings as if preparing to take off again, but Ant held a hand out to stop it. "Leave it, Brian. He's not worth it."

Mr Dawkin tried to speak, but nothing came out. Zac sort of knew how he felt. It was taking all Zac's willpower to stop himself from running screaming into the corridor.

Ant turned to Zac and Tulisa. He smiled at them, but it was a sad smile, and Zac knew what was coming next.

"I have to go now," Ant said.

Zac wanted to stop him. He didn't want Ant to leave. Not really. The bugs? Yes, he could do without those, but Ant was his friend. His *best* friend. His only friend.

"Do you?" Zac asked.

Ant nodded. "Yes. It is no longer safe for me here. I have enjoyed our friendship, Zac. I have asked Duncan to watch over you when I'm gone."

Zac frowned and said, "Who's Duncan?" Then he saw a huge fat cockroach sitting on his arm and almost fainted. "Oh … yay. Thanks," Zac squeaked.

"What if Mr Dawkin tells people about you?" Tulisa asked Ant. "They'll try to find you."

Zac, Ant and Tulisa looked over at Mr Dawkin. "He won't," Ant said. "Because there are ten quintillion insects in the world, and it'll be very easy for them to find out where Mr Dawkin lives."

Ant stepped in closer to him, and Mr Dawkin whimpered from under the webbing. "And you wouldn't want that, would you, sir?" Ant added.

Ant waited until Mr Dawkin shook his head, then he smiled. "No, I thought not," Ant said. He strolled over to the window, pulled it open and stepped up onto the ledge.

"Wait, what are you doing?" Zac asked. "Can you fly?"

"Me? Oh, no," said Ant. "But it's amazing what you can do with some help from your friends."

And with that, Ant stepped out of the window and plunged out of sight. Zac and Tulisa raced over and peered down. A cloud of flying bugs was heading towards the ground. A hand appeared from inside it. Ant's hand. It waved to them for a moment, and then the bug cloud carried on downwards.

Zac and Tulisa turned from the window. Mr Dawkin was still cocooned in webs, but there wasn't a single bug to be seen – apart from the horrible big cockroach still perched on Zac's arm.

Mr Dawkin hopped around in a circle as Zac and Tulisa walked past him. "Help me!" he begged them, in a voice muffled by the webs.

Zac and Tulisa stopped by the door. "Oh, toughen up, sir," said Tulisa.

"Yeah," said Zac. He grinned as he flicked off the light switch. "It's not like it's the end of the world!"

*

The next morning, a tickling on Zac's forehead woke him up. He groaned and tried to pull the covers over his head, but the tickling didn't go away.

"Duncan, cut it out!" Zac muttered, but the cockroach just scurried up into his hair and ran around. Zac opened his eyes and threw off his covers.

"Fine!" Zac sighed. "I'm awake. Happy?"

Duncan chirped back in a way that sounded like he was.

The morning light was creeping in under Zac's curtains. Zac lay there for a while and stared up at the ceiling. Ant was gone. Zac's friend list had dropped from one back to zero.

"Guess I'm the class weirdo again then," he said. "Right, Duncan?"

Duncan chirped.

"I'm talking to a cockroach," Zac sighed. "I'm *totally* the class weirdo."

A *thack* on the window made Zac jump in fright. He froze, his heart pounding, waiting to see if the sound was going to come again.

Thack. This time Zac saw a pebble ping off the glass.

Zac bit his lip. Someone was throwing stones at his window. But who? And why? And—

"Oh, hurry up!" a familiar voice called.

Zac slipped out of bed and crossed to the window, then opened it. Tulisa stood in his garden, her arms folded.

"Um ... what do you want?" Zac asked.

"Charming," Tulisa said. "Good morning to you too."

"Oh. Um. Yeah. Morning," said Zac. "What do you want?"

Tulisa shrugged. "I forgot to say yesterday. You did good."

"What?" Zac asked.

"You know, with the kidnapping, evil teacher and swarm of bugs stuff. You did good."

Zac nodded slowly. "Thanks. Uh, so did you."

"I know." Tulisa grinned and added, "You're all right, Zac," and then she started to turn away.

Zac watched her walking towards the gate. He saw her spot a football lying in the garden beside the path. She stopped and asked Zac, "You and Ant never did get that game of footie, did you?"

"No," Zac said. "We didn't."

Tulisa picked up the ball and tossed it from hand to hand. "Fancy a kick-about?"

Zac blinked with surprise. His friend list had just grown to one again. Duncan gave a happy chirp in his ear. Two, if Zac counted the cockroach.

"I'll be right down," Zac said.

Tulisa nodded. "I should warn you, I'm totally going to win," she said.

And she did.

Our books are tested
for children and young people by
children and young people.

Thanks to everyone who consulted on
a manuscript for their time and effort in
helping us to make our books better
for our readers.